TRASHBUS
THE BALKAN STORIES

For Tata and Mama, who fed and feed me stories. For Jürgen, because he knows why. For Maja, who read my stories and encouraged me to publish them. For all my people, whoever and wherever you may be.

Renata Britvec

TRASHBUS
THE BALKAN STORIES

Bibliographical Information of the Deutsche Nationalbibliothek
This publication is listed in the Deutsche Nationalbibliographie of
the Deutsche Nationalbibliothek; detailed bibliographical information can be accessed under http: //dnb.d-nb.de

© 2017 Renata Britvec

Cover Photo: Renata Britvec
Cover Design: Jürgen Fehrmann

Printing, Production and Layout: BoD – Books on Demand

ISBN: 978-3-7431-8222-6

Contents

How the Devil Once Paid My Grandma a Visit......7
Boat Trip Without a Cause..11
Early Frost...15
How My Uncle Met His Dog...17
Oh Jože..19
Wanna Play Frisbee?..23
Quench Your Thirst!..25
God's Dogs..29
As the River Turned Red...33
Hotel Poseidon..37
New Year's Surprise...41
The Gypsy's Blessing..45
The Gypsy's Blessing Pt. II..49
The American Traveler..53

How the Devil Once Paid
My Grandma a Visit

My grandma is a sweet old lady. She lives in this tiny Bosnian village together with my uncle and spends most of her time in the garden. Besides from enjoying her time outdoors and taking care of my uncle's various pets, she likes to garden. There's peppermint growing, and cherry tomatoes, and all kinds of flowers like roses, begonias, hortensias, red and yellow gladiolas, some types of orchid, oleander, and grapevine. Up the hill in the more unkempt part of my family's lot, my grandma grows giant cabbages, zucchini, peppers, big juicy tomatoes, strawberries, onions, potatoes and other vegetables. She waters the plants, clears them of weeds, talks to them and makes them feel comfortable.

On rainy days and in winter, she likes to watch Mexican telenovelas and some Turkish series. Sometimes she has coffee with the neighbors. She likes to eat candy and cake. And she loves lubenica – watermelon. When I was a child I used to persuade her to have a cigarette with her coffee because I thought it looked funny when she smoked. Most of the time, she had done me the favor. She's physically fit, although she has slowed down quite a bit, and mentally she is stable even if she has weird thoughts sometimes, but I guess most old ladies have strange ideas every now and then.

So, a couple of years ago, one day in late summer, my grandma was sitting in the living room, knitting. The days were getting colder so she preferred to stay inside, but she kept the window tilted to have some fresh air. She concentrated on her knitting but every once in a while heard something, a crackling noise from next to the cupboard. At first, she thought it was nothing. But as the rustling sounds wouldn't stop, she called my uncle and my grandpa, who was still alive back then, to tell them there was something wrong. The two men were irritated as nothing was to be heard and shrugged it off as the figment of an old lady's imagination. The rustling re-appeared after they had left the room and my grandma was getting nervous.

It was getting late and when it finally was time to go to bed, my grandma at first didn't dare switch off the light. She sleeps in the living room; and she was scared the noises might come back. She became more and more tired though, forgot about the sounds, turned out the light after all and fell asleep.

In the middle of the night, my uncle and my grandpa woke up alarmed by my grandma's screams of horror.

"Đavo sjedi na ormaru i gleda u mene!" she was yelling.

"The devil is sitting on top of the cupboard and he's looking at me!"

He supposedly had red, glow-in-the-dark eyes and wanted to steal my grandmother's soul. My uncle and my grandpa couldn't see him. Apparently, he had already vanished. They searched the cupboard and the whole of the room and couldn't find anything or anyone. They decided to go back to bed, for if the devil really wanted to do business, he would return some other time. Grandma spent the rest of the night with the lights on, saying some prayers, because that surely wouldn't do any harm.

The next day, my uncle was chatting with a neighbor outside in the garden, beneath the living room window, next to the big apple tree. The branches and leaves of the tree reach directly to the window, and if you want to close it, you have to move the leaves first, so they don't get jammed. While my uncle was talking to the neighbor, he noticed some commotion in the treetop. He looked up and saw a squirrel squeeze through the tilted window and hop onto the crown of the tree.

Boat Trip Without a Cause

I was staying at my uncle's place in Bosnia for ten days when my cousin decided to come and visit us for the weekend. My cousin is my uncle's son, but he lives with his mother's family in Serbia. It was really hot the weekend he came and we wanted to go swimming at a lake, but my uncle had a better idea. He told us about a boat he kept in the basement. It was supposed to be comfortable and super-fast. It had a motor so we could speed over the lake instead of just swim. It sounded like the RMS Queen Mary's little sister.

The next day after breakfast we went to the basement to get the boat ready. My uncle pulled out the boat from the basement and we had a closer look. It was a rubber boat with some wood on the bottom to keep it stable, and it had a small outboard motor which my uncle had somehow managed to install. God only knows how he had come up with the idea and how he had succeeded with it.

The boat was dirty yellow. I blinked. My cousin said nothing. A black long-legged spider crawled out from underneath one of the rubber folds. We put the boat into the trunk of the car and drove to the lake; it took us about half an hour.

It was noon when we arrived at the lake. We got out of the car and got the boat out of the trunk. It was incredibly hot outside and I was worried that we would get sunstroke after an hour tops. My uncle and my cousin inflated the boat and then my uncle remembered he had forgotten the paddles at home. The air shimmered with heat and everything glistened.

"Well, I guess we don't need them really, the boat has a motor after all," I said.

"We need the paddles to get off the shore so I can start the motor. You two stay here while I go and get the paddles," my uncle said. And took off.

There we were. The lake was polluted. There was trash all around the shore and dead fish.

"So, what are we gonna do? Should we go swimming?" my cousin asked.

"Hell no! I won't. Let's just wait. He'll be back," I said.

"Yeah. You're probably right. I don't feel like swimming, either."

I took a look around. There were no trees or bushes, so there was no protecting shadow. Instead, there was a huge boat, rather a ship, which had rusted completely and was filled with empty bottles. It must have been the community's trash can. I took a couple of pictures of the trash-ship and the dead fish.

"Šta imaš to slikati?" my cousin asked me. He thought it was stupid to take photos of ugly things.

My uncle came back with only one paddle. One paddle was of no use. So that was that. We tried to get the boat into the water deep enough to start the motor. The boat was tiny. There was not enough room for the three of us to sit on opposite sides, so we had to lie next to each other in a row, packed like sardines, with our feet dangling in the dirty water. My uncle started the motor and off we went. It was fun. We sped across the lake and drops of water sprayed our legs and faces. The fun lasted about two minutes when the motor broke.

As my uncle can't swim so well with his war-injured leg, he told my cousin and me to get off the boat and pull it back to the shore.

Now the problem had to be solved. I don't have the slightest idea about how to fix a motor, so I kept my mouth shut. The two men were discussing how to go about it. They needed some part or tool my uncle didn't have. I wanted them to give up and go back home and go to a public swimming pool, but I didn't dare say anything. My uncle noticed this man close to where we had stranded and the guy gave him the tool he needed. While my uncle was fixing the motor, I was thinking.

"But ... don't you think this will happen again? I mean, what if we're in the middle of the lake and the motor breaks again?" I asked.

"It won't happen again."

The motor seemed to be fixed and we took off one more time. Directly towards the middle of the huge lake, with a slight left hand twist towards the area where the shore is steep and there are woods. We were far out when the motor broke down. Again my cousin and I had to jump into the water and try to pull the boat towards the shore. But I couldn't. I didn't have the strength. Not only was the shore too far away, it wouldn't have been possible for my uncle to climb it because it was too steep, and we couldn't have saved the boat.

Then a lake taxi came by. The guy on the taxi, which was a real boat, saved us. We tied the rubber boat to the taxi, my uncle stayed in the boat and my cousin and I had to somehow climb into the taxi. I don't know how I did it, there were no stairs, no ladder, no rope. There was no help for me. It took me ten minutes to get in there. I was embarrassed.

After we had changed, deflated the boat and put it back inside the trunk, my uncle took us to a bar at the lake to treat us to cold drinks. We were sitting there, smoking, and while my uncle was discussing something important with my cousin, I was contemplating the pirate ship outside the bar at the shore. It looked wrecked.

On our way back home we saw a gypsy boy riding his bike. My uncle made fun of him because the kid had tried to dye his hair blond but it had turned out orange.

Early Frost

When my uncle had returned back home from the hospital, not a lot of people came to visit for quite a long time. He had to stay in bed several months and was too weak to do anything, really. My grandparents were taking care of him; basically, every day was the same to him. One day a cat came along. She was a black, mean thing, but she apparently took a liking to my uncle and stayed to live with him while he was recovering from his war injury.

As time passed by, the cat had babies. Her babies had babies, and so on. At some point, about seventeen cats were populating my grandma's garden. Strictly speaking, they were all wild cats, but the garden was their headquarters, and my uncle looked after them and fed them regularly. The neighbors weren't happy about the cats strolling through their gardens, stealing meat and cake from the tables, and my grandma didn't like the situation, either. But there was nothing much she or anybody could do because the cats were under my uncle's protection.

Now, my mother goes to Bosnia a lot to visit my uncle and my grandma, especially since my dad died, her dad died, and she retired. While she's there, I try to call often to check on everybody's well-being. So one day in early March I called. Our conversation was the same as every time when I phone my grandma's place. My mother was telling me about the weather, about how nothing much was happening in the little village. People were growing old, they rarely visited each other anymore. My uncle was unwell; the weather was making his leg hurt.

I asked about the animals. The dog was fine but wouldn't leave his hutch because he didn't like the weather, either. The bird was still in the house. It was too early yet to take it back outside to its aviary in the garden. It was singing away and giving my mother trouble because she had to clean after it all the time. It liked to throw stuff out of its cage. The cats seemed to be OK, too, but my mother didn't mention them, so I asked her.

One of the kittens was gone. I wanted to know what had happened. My uncle had noticed the kitten had been missing. It hadn't been among its siblings when he'd wanted to feed them. That was quite unusual, but he had thought that maybe the kitten was taking a stroll through the nearby woods or perhaps was playing in the neighbor's garden. He had kept looking for it throughout the day, but it kept missing.

Next morning, they found the kitten. It was drowned and frozen in the neighbor's rain barrel. They could see its body through the thin layer of ice.

How My Uncle Met His Dog

My uncle lives in a small village in the mountainous region of central Bosnia. He's a war veteran, and as he can't work anymore, he has a lot of spare time and nothing much to do. He keeps himself busy with stuff that has to be done around the house, but he also likes to spend time with the other weird men from the village. Most of them are his age or a bit older, most of them are missing teeth. Some of them are working, but all are pretty much in the same situation.

Besides from hanging out in cafés and bars, having coffee or coca cola, they meet up to play cards sometimes. The card games usually take place in a Bosnian-style sort of community center, which is just a shack up on a mountain close to my uncle's place. There are no decent roads but only rocky paths up the mountain, yet my uncle somehow manages to drag the old car up and down these tracks every day without wrecking it completely.

One night he's done with playing cards and wants to drive back home. Smoking and listening to some gypsy tunes, he's bumping along the curvy path. At the same time, the dog is going for a walk, and at some point, he crosses my uncle's path. When he sees my uncle's car coming, he just stands still and therefore forces my uncle to stop the car because the road is so narrow my uncle can't avoid the dog.

My uncle has it with animals. He's like the extended version of the horse whisperer. The dog, on the other hand, is some mythical creature, or at least he looks like one. He sports the air of a werewolf, but a pretty dandy one. I think he does that on purpose because really, he's just a typical Serbian sheepdog from the mountains, a so-called Šarplaninac. Nobody knows if the dog had run away or where exactly he came from, he just simply appeared in the village, taking strolls around the surrounding mountains.

So anyways, my uncle gets out of the car and talks to the dog a bit, trying to explain the dog has to move so he can drive back home. The dog finally understands and lets my uncle pass. The same thing happens one more time a couple of days later. The third time they meet, my uncle suggests they should live together. The dog seems to be OK with it, but he won't get in the car. So my uncle drives home real slow, and the dog paces along right next to the car until they finally reach my uncle's and my grandma's house.

I think my uncle leashed the dog until the next morning. Then he divided the estate around the house in two parts, put up a fence and gave one part to the dog. He also built him a dog-hutch. The dog has been living with him for more than seven years now. He's taking care of my grandma when my uncle's not at home.

Oh Jože!

My dad's dad, grandpa Nikola, must have been a funny character. He died the year I was born, so I never had the chance to meet him. I only know my dad's stories about his dad.

My grandpa's nickname was Mika. He liked to party. He liked going out with his friends, he enjoyed music, singing and dancing. And he sure liked his rakija. Šljivovica was his favorite, a sort of Croatian plum brandy. As far as I know, he was a bit vain, too. To my grandma's sorrow, he spent a lot of money on drinks and hairspray.

My dad was already a young man, but his younger sisters and brothers were teenagers and they were still living at my grandparents' house. One night, Mika had a friend over. My grandma Barbara didn't like Mika having guys come to their house, because they bugged her when they got drunk and started telling silly stories or, even worse, switched to talking about the really important things in life. She couldn't stand them. Actually, she often couldn't stand Mika either. That's why she always went to visit a neighbor when my grandpa had company.

So, Mika was alone with his friend and his four youngest children. The kids were real rascals and liked to tease Mika whenever possible. They were in their room, the one next to the living room where Mika and his friend Jože were drinking their rakija. The kids were telling each other jokes, simply having fun, giggling and laughing. It was already late and Mika was getting drunk and a bit touchy. The laughter coming from the room next door annoyed him. He wanted to talk to Jože in peace. Besides, the kids should have been sleeping. So he went to their room and told them to shut up and go to sleep. But the kids wouldn't listen. They kept making noise, being happy about how easy it was to infuriate their dad. Mika got really angry and jumped into their room one more time, threatening them with some sort of punishment.

The kids knew he was on the edge of losing it. But they couldn't stop now, no way! So they put my grandma Bara's wooden washtub on one of the beds, other stuff on the other bed – they were four kids but had to share two beds – and covered everything up with pillows and blankets so it looked like they were in their beds. Then they hid underneath and started screaming and laughing hysterically to provoke Mika even more. Oh and how they provoked him.

Mika was furious. He grabbed some wooden plank or rod or something similar, tore open the door to the kids' room and started swinging at the washtub like crazy, yelling and cursing. He was a bit drunk which is why it took him so long to realize the children weren't in their beds. When he found out, he also realized he had broken Bara's washtub and started hollering:

"Ooooo Jože, ubiće me Bara! Vidi šta mi je banda napravila!"

Now he was scared his wife was gonna kill him because he had broken her only washtub and he was even angrier, because of course all of this was the childrens' fault! Jože – thank God the man was quick-witted – pulled my grandpa away from the kids. They instantly seized the opportunity, fled from the house and hid in the barn until my grandma came back home.

Mika anticipated my grandma's rage, attacked her and told her:

"Look what devils you have given birth to, they made me break your washtub."

I don't know if he really got away with it. But even if he did on this occasion, there were many more on which my grandma made his life a living hell.

Wanna Play Frisbee?

My dad was excellent at improvising. When he was a kid he didn't have any toys, so he invented or built some for himself and his friends.

One day, the kids of the village had heard of a miraculous disc they could throw into the air, and it would glide through it until another kid caught it. You could throw the disc back and forth, and it was more elegant and modern than just playing with a ball. I have no idea how the kids had found out about the frisbee. It was invented only in 1948 in the USA, so it was quite a novelty when my dad was a kid.

His family didn't own a TV set, so the children hadn't seen cool American guys playing frisbee on-screen. I doubt that the other kids' parents had a TV either. Maybe they had heard about it on the radio, or maybe one of their relatives from the city or some foreign country had told them about it.

My dad wanted to play frisbee, but he didn't have one. He was thinking about how to get hold of one. He had no money. And there was no way his mom would have bought him one.

So he came up with an idea and told his friends about it. He was sure that the cut-out lid of a can would serve them just well enough. My dad and the other kids looked for old cans and cut the lids off and tried which one was flying best. After they had chosen one, they positioned themselves on the meadow and started playing.

My dad wanted to be the first to play with the newly acquired toy and started throwing it back and forth with one of his friends. The edge of the lid was frayed, and the can lid-frisbee was hard to catch. Neither my dad nor his friend dared catch it, so they were just throwing it and, disappointingly, it fell to the ground, and they had to pick it up again. But they continued playing nonetheless.

My dad's friend threw the lid one more time, and it landed on my dad's face. The fringed edge of the can lid split his upper lip. My dad had a small but prominent scar on his upper lip for the rest of his life.

Quench Your Thirst!

It was a hot summer day in the small Croatian village where my dad grew up. Two of his kid sisters, they were about twelve and ten years old, were working in the cowshed as their mother had told them to. They were sweating and cursing; not only was it unbearably hot, but the smell was taking their breath away, too. It was late afternoon and they were hoping for their dad to come back home soon, for he would definitely allow them to put aside the pitchforks and go swimming.

At that time, my grandpa was working in the city during the week and only came back home for the weekends. The family was poor, he didn't earn much. The little he earned, he liked to spend with his friends after a week of hard work. He liked to sing and dance, my grandpa. Nevertheless, each Friday he went to a store in the city and got something for the kids. Little things, nothing special. Maybe some salami or a wedge of cheese, or chocolate, and in summer he bought Cockta for the kids. Cockta is the Yugoslav version of Coca Cola, although the recipe is quite different. It has a bitter-sweet taste to it. Back then, you could buy Cockta only in those small bottles, and my Grandpa had bought one for each kid, so there were eight bottles in his bag when he returned home that day.

My aunts were clearing the dung out of the cowshed as the younger one spotted her dad on the road to the house. She threw away the dungfork and ran towards him to be the first to greet him and see what gifts he had brought for them. My aunt Jagoda was a lively little creature when she was a kid. She was witty, but she could be a devil, too. She had a pig she had trained so she could ride it, just for fun. She knew how to get what she wanted.

So she ran towards my grandpa and greeted him in the sweetest possible way. Of course he was aware that she was only looking to get something out of his bag, and so he gave her a bottle of Cockta. But Jagoda told him she was working in the shed with Ljiljana and that it might be a good idea if my grandpa gave her another bottle so she could surprise her older sister. My grandpa gave her another bottle and Jagoda ran away back to the shed.

She hid behind the corner and finished her bottle in one big gulp. The original Cockta bottles are really small. She was still thirsty and finished the other one, too. Now that the damage was done, she figured she could play a trick on her sister because now it didn't matter anyway. Around the cowshed there was a ditch for the liquid shit and piss to drain off. Jagoda kneeled down, always careful as to not be seen by her sister, and filled the Cockta bottle with the liquid manure. It had about the same color as Cockta. What had spilled, she wiped off with her skirt.

When she entered the cowshed, her sister was dizzy with heat and from the smell. Jagoda told her she had a surprise – their dad had sent her a bottle of ice-cold Cockta, too. It was dark in the cowshed and my aunt Ljiljana was close to dying of thirst, so before even noticing something was wrong, she took a big gulp of liquid manure.

Ljiljana and Jagoda spent the rest of the evening chasing each other around the cowshed and the lot. I do not know if Ljiljana ever got a hold of Jagoda to beat the shit out of her, but probably not. Jagoda had always been the smarter one, and she was faster, too.

God's Dogs

One summer, I was still a teenager back then, my parents decided to go to Marija Bistrica for Assumption Day. Marija Bistrica is a Croatian place of pilgrimage about 30 miles from Zagreb. The Virgin Mary had appeared to a girl there one day a long time ago, and that's why the small, unimportant village had turned into a religious place.

I had never been to Marija Bistrica before, and although I didn't consider myself religious, I figured it might be fun to get out of the city and go on a trip with my parents. I was a bit disappointed when they asked my uncle and his wife, who back then were living in our house, to come along. I didn't like my aunt. Him I didn't like that much either, but granted he could be funny. He had a small white dog with which he shared his bed instead of with his wife. In general, my uncle Matija was an unpleasant person with a temper. He was grumpy and red-faced.

Matija's wife didn't want to go so it was just the four of us. When we arrived, my dad found a parking space pretty quickly and we wandered through what felt like millions of people to the outdoor church. It was hot outside and really crowded. I think the entire Croatian population had congregated to go to Mass.

Matija was fidgeting. He told my parents he wanted to have a look around. He didn't want to stay with us for Mass. So my parents told him where to meet afterwards. They wanted to listen to Mass without ruffle or excitement, so they were happy with Matija leaving.

After Mass, we picked up Matija at the arranged meeting point and went shopping. There were stalls selling religious souvenirs and plastic stuff for kids. Matija bought a huge wooden crucifix. The woman at the stall had wanted to put it into a bag, but Matija had refused to take the bag and now was carrying the crucifix in his hand.

My dad was hungry and wanted to eat. There were various market stalls offering sandwiches and other food, and of course there were hundreds of butchers who had brought their meat and equipment for barbecue. My dad loved grilled meat.

The thing is, these market stalls and barbecues are pretty improvised. They're outdoors, you know, and there's just plastic chairs and tables or ale-benches, and the plates and cutlery are plastic, too. It's a typical Balkan get-together, there's crowds of people, so everything is a bit messy and yeah, let's admit it, a bit dirty, too. Now, these miserable conditions annoyed Matija. He was already upset about how there were no table cloths and proper cutlery. No matter where we wanted to sit, he would start screaming NO! because he was disgusted.

After about half an hour of looking for a place to Matija's taste, my dad ran out of energy and just sat down at a table and ordered food. He was fed up with his brother's perpetual nagging. He told Matija to go find a restaurant with proper tables and white table cloths and silver cutlery – he by all means would definitely not move one inch further before eating. Matija ran away mad as hell, but as he depended on us to bring him back home, he was keeping us in sight.

We finished our food calmly, paid and took off towards the parking lot. Matija caught up with us. It seemed as if everybody wanted to leave at the exact same time. I was getting a bit nervous, too, because there were so many people and now I was a bit scared I would lose my parents and never find my way back home because I sure as hell would not be able to find the car, either. So I was clinging to my mom desperately, trying to keep pace with her and not to be carried off my feet by the hordes of people, when suddenly Matija started yelling like crazy.

"Bog ti mater jebo, ko te pusti da hodaš kud narod hoda!"

He was hitting a big dog with his big wooden crucifix while screaming and shouting like a madman. He cursed the dog, and he cursed God and the dog's owner for letting the dog walk where people were walking. The poor creature had tried to make its way through the crowds, too, and had accidentally brushed my uncle's pants, which made Matija snap because now his pants were as dirty as the rest of that goddamned place.

The whole world was looking at us in this moment, deeply shocked. My dad, although used to that kind of behavior, was embarrassed. He shut his brother up and pulled him away from the dog, brought him to the car, sat him inside and told him to keep calm. But Matija kept on about how he was hungry and how disgusting everything had been and how this stupid dog had annoyed him. All the way back home, my dad was making fun of him, laughing with my mother.

Back at home, Matija took out my dad's barbecue and prepared sausages, which he ate alone outside in the garden. Actually, his dog kept him company.

As the River Turned Red

All through the war, my parents took me there. To our house in Croatia. In the beginning I was skeptical, but I was a kid, and what the hell did I know. I also thought all this was kind of exciting. An adventure. Theoretically, I was aware that the borders could be closed any minute and that we might be trapped. But I didn't understand what that meant. I thought that if we got trapped, we would go to the German embassy and have them save us. But we weren't Germans. We are not German.

I was scared my dad would be forced to join the army or some paramilitary unit in the woods in the village, where he comes from, and then he would have to wear a uniform or a camouflage colored military outfit and carry a rifle or a gun and he would have to shoot. At the Front. At the river Kupa.

My parents told me that we would be listening to the radio constantly and if anything pointed to an aggravation of the situation we would leave Croatia immediately, and as we were pretty close to the Slovenian border, it shouldn't be a problem. They wanted to look after the family. I understand. I understood. I wanted to see my family, too. So we went there for every holiday and vacation.

One day we drove to one of those villages south of Zagreb to visit my grandma and my uncle Mirko and my aunt Milica. Mirko had a bar, Milica was running a hair salon. Milica had successfully talked me into letting her give me a perm. She was a voluptuous woman. She had brown hair, big hair, big, dreamy eyes, big lashes, big lips, big tits, big hips, a big butt, big legs. She always looked unhappy, in a tragic way. Even back then I understood that. I think it's because she couldn't have kids. My parents told me she was unable to conceive. She used to ask me if I was prone to gain weight and I disliked her because of that.

I was also angry because every time Milica met my grandmother, my mother's mother, the Bosnian grandmother, she asked her if my grandma could tell her fortune by reading the coffee grounds. Now, my Bosnian family is super-Catholic and a world away from any kind of witchcraft or other sorts of monkey business-magic. So anyways, Milica chemically treated my hair while she was chattering with one of her regular customers. They were talking about the war and about a guy who had been killed. They knew him.

"To ti je sveta smrt," the woman said.

She thought it was a blessed death, because he had been shot to death and nothing bad had happened to him. I was listening to them, all eyes and ears. There was nothing I could have said at that moment. I just blinked. I thought I had learned something important from this conversation. I had learned about holiness. I had learned what a blessed death was. I felt I should be sure to remember this.

Back at home, at night, my parents were discussing something in the upper hall which leads to their bedroom and my bedroom and one other room. My parents were talking about some people who had got shot and I had the impression that finally finally the moment had come in which I could contribute to the conversation and share something meaningful and I repeated:

"To je sveta smrt!"

I was utterly convinced I was speaking the truth, telling them something they hadn't been aware of so far. Pause. They looked at each other. Then they looked at me.

"Da, dijete drago, pa stvarno, joj," they said.

Yes, dear child, really, oh, that's true. I don't know what they were thinking at that moment. I went to my room.

It was getting late, night had begun. It was dark. I got ready to go to bed. I said good night to everybody and wanted to go to sleep. I don't know how much time had passed when I heard the gunfire. Gunfire is really loud and it can be heard at a distance of more than 20 miles. I listened. And I listened. And I wondered what was going on and I knew what was going on but I didn't know. And I wondered how far away the gunshots really were. And it seemed to me they must come from another world. And I was lying in my bed while the river Kupa was turning red.

Hotel Poseidon

During the war, my parents still went to Croatia whenever possible to check on our family. They took me along most of the time. It must have been in 1992 or 1993, I was about twelve years old, when my mother and father decided to go on a vacation on the Adriatic. As it was too dangerous to travel through the country, they chose to spend the vacation in the North, in Istria, close to the Slovenian, Austrian and Italian borders. Just in case. Usually, we would travel further down South and spend our summers somewhere in Dalmatia. Also, we never stayed at hotels. My parents didn't like planning our vacations, so we just hopped in the car, drove South, picked a place and asked around for private accommodation.

That year though my dad thought it would be a good idea to try and stay at a hotel. As it was wartime, the prices for rooms were really low. My dad had heard of this pretty city of Poreč and wanted to go there, so that's where we went. When we arrived in Poreč, my dad stopped at a tourist information center and asked about accommodation. They sent him to Hotel Poseidon.

The staff at the hotel was nice. Still I felt awkward because I had never stayed at a hotel before and everything was so big, the entrance hall, the restaurant, the chairs even. People were dressed in suits, which seemed weird to me, because it was nice and hot. The staff showed us to our rooms. I had my own room and my parents left me there so they could unpack their stuff.

The view was nice. Right outside the room there was the harbor, and I could smell the sea and the rotting fish and I watched the boats swaying on the water and I heard the seagulls cry. I checked everything out, the bathroom, the closet, the TV. I didn't know what to make of the place, it felt strange to me. I felt uncomfortable, closed in. It smelled weird, too.

My parents picked me up when they were done and we spent the rest of the day at the beach. There weren't many people around, mostly Croatians and some other tourists. There was a war going on in the country, after all. We were happy, though. In the evening, we had dinner at the hotel, and after taking a walk through the old town, my parents wanted to go to sleep. They brought me to my room and left. I didn't want to be alone. And the weird smell was still there. I didn't know what to do, really. I tried to ignore it and went to bed. But in bed the smell was worse. It came from the bed. I didn't sleep at all until morning.

Next day, I told my parents about the smell. Now, my parents are cool people, but like everybody else, they have their flaws. They didn't believe me. It wasn't possible that something was wrong with the room. Their logic was: If the people at the hotel, who are educated and well-informed, let the room to tourists, the room must be OK. Otherwise they wouldn't put guests in there. They felt it would be impolite to ask the staff to check the room.

That night, I once again tried to ignore the smell, but I thought it had gotten even worse. That was probably just my imagination running wild, but still, that's the way I felt. The third or fourth day I forced my parents to take a closer look – rather whiff – because I couldn't stand it anymore. And then they finally noticed the stench. It was urine. They talked to the concierge and I got another room.

At the beginning of the war and especially during winter, the hotel had to give shelter to refugees from war zones. There were a lot of people from all over Croatia, and I think also from Bosnia, who had been brought to the hotel. Those people came from places of terror. Their homes had been destroyed; they had nowhere else to go. All their shattered lives, their fear and their despair had been in these hotel rooms. Until they had to go to other places so the hotel could open up for the few tourists who were to arrive in summer.

New Year's Surprise

My parents wanted to celebrate Christmas in Croatia and decided to spend New Year's there, too. The war was only just over. Back then, my uncle Matija was still living in our house with his family. There was my aunt, her mother, and my two cousins, a boy and a girl. My parents also invited uncle Mario and his wife and kid over to celebrate New Year's. Fortunately, my cousin and I were allowed to invite some friends over, too.

I was excited, because I was at the age when parties start to become interesting, mostly because of the boys at the parties, alcohol maybe, and everything else that seems so seductive about staying up the whole night. There's a promise in it, and you don't know what that promise is, but you feel it and it's big and it smiles at you and tells you everything is possible and you will witness something grand.

My girl cousin, she's a year older than me but back then seemed so much more experienced and mature, invited some of her girlfriends and some boys, too. I was super-nervous and started to think about what I would wear that evening days before the party. I was convinced I would meet a cute guy and dance the night away and get kissed. I was a hundred percent sure.

In the afternoon of that special last day of the year, we started preparing my cousin's room for the party.

We moved the furniture, set up a table with snacks and drinks. The room looked pitiful. I don't know what I had expected, but I was unhappy because it still looked like her room. We put up a cassette recorder. My cousin only had cassettes. I had brought some of my music, too, Michael Jackson mostly, and was hoping we would also listen to my stuff so I could show off how cool I was.

It was getting late and my cousin's friends started arriving at the party. Some girls I knew already, some I didn't know, but they were all OK. But I think it was only three or four girls. We waited a bit and I hoped more people would show up, but nobody came. No more girls, and not a single boy. I was somewhat disappointed, sad. I was wearing a short black velvet dress with see-through chiffon sleeves and black high heels. I just had hit puberty. And it was the nineties, after all. But nobody would see me in my dress now anyway.

The girls were really nice, and they were fun, too. So we just made the best of the evening. We listened to Croatian pop songs, had a couple of drinks – well, to be honest, I didn't, back then I hated the taste of alcohol – danced and sang along to the music. One girl asked me if I could send her hip t-shirts when I got back to Germany and she would pay me next time we met or she could send me the money. It was almost 12 p. m. and everybody was getting excited.

And then there were gunshots and all the girls started screaming and hiding underneath the tables and chairs. It happened so quickly I didn't know how to react and I was still smiling. And I didn't know whether I should laugh because they looked ridiculous, or if maybe I should hide, too. I think I was the one who looked like an idiot, the only one standing up in her dress. I asked what was going on and one girl answered, her fear and her blank brown eyes answered me.

"There's gunfire outside!"

And then somebody else, I think it was my cousin, dared to peek through the window and said it was only my uncle Mario celebrating New Year's. It had just turned midnight and he had taken his air gun outside and was shooting into the night sky in our dark backyard where the hedgehog lives.

He was standing right in front of our window. My parents excused themselves in place of my uncle. They were sorry the girls got scared, but everybody calmed down quickly. We continued celebrating, but only for a short time. Soon after midnight the girls had to go home because their parents wouldn't allow them to stay up all night.

When my cousin and I got up the next day, my aunt, uncle and my parents started interrogating us. If we had liked our party, if we had fun, and so on. My uncle looked angry, my parents were smirking. I didn't really understand what the hell they wanted and what was so funny? It was a party, yes, we had fun, everybody went home and that was that. Then they started asking about the alcohol. I said I hadn't been drinking, and as usual, nobody would believe me. My cousin didn't say anything. But when she realized the adults wouldn't stop asking questions, she admitted she had had a glass or two of champagne and it had made her sick.

After the other girls had left, she went straight to the bathroom and vomited into the sink; she couldn't make it to the toilet, that's how sick she felt. And as the vomit clogged the drain and she didn't know what else to do, she put a towel over the sink and covered everything up. When my uncle Matija, her dad, woke up and wanted to use the bathroom, he got sick because of the smell and was pretty disgusted when he found his New Year's surprise in the sink.

The Gypsy's Blessing

A couple of years after the war, after all my aunts and uncles and cousins and grandmas had moved back to their own homes, my parents wanted to refurbish our house. At one point during the war, more than fifteen people had lived there. Everything was run down, especially the kitchen. My parents threw everything out and ordered new furniture. They only held on to the old electric stove, because it was still running and they needed it to prepare food while the kitchen was being renovated.

They put the old stove into the storeroom, and that's where they cooked. From the first day the stove had been moved, one of my dad's sisters kept asking what was going to happen to the stove and if my parents really, really still needed it. She lived in the same city and came by often. Sometimes she just called to check. She also told my dad that his brother would take the stove, and even his brother-in-law would accept the old thing to make room in the house for my parents.

The new furniture had arrived and a whole year had passed. The stove was still in the storeroom. My mother enjoyed her new and clean kitchen. She was preparing lunch; my dad was sitting at the kitchen table, smoking and thinking. He left the room and didn't come back for quite a while. My mom noticed that he had disappeared, but she wasn't worried. My dad sometimes did that. He rarely let you know what he was up to.

After a while, my mom looked through the window and saw my dad coming back from the meadow across from our house. Back then, there still was the meadow where I used to play endless afternoons with my friends and my little dog. It was rather big, the meadow, and I always had a nice view from out of my window. Now there's an enormous, red, Austrian supermarket. It's called Billa. Now that's my view.

My dad was coming back to the house accompanied by two gypsies. A middle-aged guy and a kid about fifteen years old. Those gypsies had their camp in the woods close to the city. When they had some business to do in town, they used to leave their horse-drawn carriage in the meadow across from our house. Their horses could feed there, too.

My dad brought the two men to the house and introduced them to my mom.

"Here, I thought I could show these two gentlemen our old stove, and if they like it, they can have it."

My mom nodded. She opened the door to the storeroom, and the man inspected the stove happily.

"Joj, super šporet! Hoču! Odo po kola!" he said.

He thought it was pretty impressive and wanted to go get the carriage because the stove would have been too heavy for him and his son to carry all the way back to the other end of the meadow.

Father and son went to get their horses and cart, and when they returned, my dad helped them to load the stove onto the cart. My dad wished the man all the best.

"May you grow old and use this stove to cook for you and your family as long as you live!" he said.

The gypsy in return blessed my dad's soul and wandered off with the stove, which now was forever lost to my family.

The Gypsy's Blessing Pt. II

We were visiting my mom in Zagreb. One day, we decided to climb the Medvednica mountain. Which was ridiculously insane, a suicide commando, because it was 40 degrees Celsius outside, but that's another story. We left rather early in the morning and came back late. When we got home, barely able to walk anymore, sweaty, smelly, hungry, thirsty and tired, my mom treated us to her delicious homemade food. After dinner, we were playing in the garden and hosed each other down. Then my friend wanted to go to bed. I just took a shower and went back downstairs to chat with my mother. Here's what she told me about what happened after we had left for our excursion:

We had left to explore Medvednica, and my mom was doing stuff around the house. As she didn't know when we would be back, she started preparing food for dinner already in the early afternoon. She likes to be well prepared, my mom. She had had lunch outside and left the table and chairs there for dinner.

My mom was in the kitchen cooking, the window open. At some point she noticed a gypsy girl coming towards our house. The girl was pregnant. And she was carrying scarfs and blankets she wanted to sell in the neighborhood.

The girl was looking at my mom through the open window and was walking straight towards her. She opened the gate, entered our garden and went directly to the window at which my mom was standing.

She asked my mom if she wanted to buy something, but my mom didn't need a scarf. She said no.

"Aj mi skuvaj kavu!"

The girl wanted her to make her a cup of coffee.

"Come on, make me a cup of coffee, I'll go and sit at the table outside, over there."

My mom was thinking. She even would have offered the girl a cup, cause she was pregnant, and in the Balkans, nobody turns their head after pregnant women drinking coffee, it's no big deal there. But she didn't want her to hang out in the garden and distract her. So my mother thought of a compromise and offered her a glass of water. She gave it to the girl through the window and told her she didn't have time for coffee because she was waiting for her children to come back home and needed to prepare food.

"Daj da ti ogledam," the girl offered.

She was about to read my mother's future. But my mom didn't want her to.

"Oh. You don't believe in witchcraft, do you? No. You believe in God. In this case, I can't tell your fortune."

But the girl had something to say, anyway.

"Listen. I can't tell your fortune, but I will advise you about one thing. Listen to me carefully. There is a woman. She's a widow, and she is right here in this town where you and your daughter are. And she wishes you and your daughter ill. Be careful! Look out! She is going especially after your daughter. But she won't be able to do her any harm because your daughter is being protected by God."

My mom told her that she was sure that God was protecting me – after all, she prays for me every day – and the girl said goodbye and left.

Granted this is a weird story and I didn't dare tell anybody so far. But I must admit that now that some time has passed and I remember the story, it's damn fine to know I'm under somebody's or something's protection.

The American Traveler

We had been in Dubrovnik a couple of days already when we met the American traveler. My friend and I had been to a war museum in the old town and after being exposed to pictures of horror and grief we didn't know what to do but to go and have a drink. We went to the Art Café which was on the way to our apartment. There were no tables available, so I asked a guy who was sitting by himself if we could join him. He didn't mind.

My friend and I just ordered drinks but didn't talk. We were sitting there for a while in silence when the guy asked us if we were Croatian. So I answered yes, I was. We started talking and I explained I lived in Berlin, just like my friend, and that we were in Dubrovnik on a vacation. The American was not on a vacation. He was a long-term traveler; he had been living with gypsies in the Czech Republic for a while, fighting in boxing matches, before he came to Croatia to travel some more in Europe. He was to return to the States soon because he had run out of money.

We arranged to meet the following day to go to one of the beaches at the west end of the city where there weren't too many people. It was located in a small bay. My friend is not a good swimmer. He really needed a vacation, he needed to rest, to sleep and to be by himself. He needed to drink. I was in another mood. I wanted something. I don't know. I probably wanted to dissolve.

My friend stayed at the beach, sleeping, and the American took me swimming. We swam to the other side of the bay where there were some caves. We explored one. It was small and there was not much to see really, but in front of the cave there were huge rocks, so it felt like swimming in a bathtub, which was fun. At the entrance to the cave, the water was shallow and almost hot. The American knew I liked the sea and he gave me the skeleton of an urchin he had found in the cave. Due to the weird construction of rocks surrounding the cave entrance, the water was stagnant. There were millions of mosquitoes and after a while, I couldn't stand being bitten anymore.

We left the cave and went swimming in the bay. The American was a free-diver. He was diving while I was just swimming or floating in the salty water, feeling the sun on my face. I like to look at the sun with my eyes closed because then there is only orange and red and a bit yellow and it feels warm.

The American came back from the sea bed with a huge shell he had found for me. It was empty already and dead, so he brought it up to the sunlight. It was all mossy and green and kind of mucous, and I was stunned. I took it carefully and we swam to the shore and climbed up the hill to where the path was. Some guys we met on the way told us to be careful not to get caught, because it is illegal to take shells out of the sea.

We tried to walk back to my friend quickly and without being noticed, and when we arrived I wrapped the shell in my clothes so I could take it back to our apartment without breaking it to pieces.

My friend had to leave for Berlin the next day and I had to go to Bosnia the day after. I spent my last day in Dubrovnik with the American traveler. We went on an island cruise where again we went swimming and diving and swimming and looking for stuff in the sea.

In Bosnia, my uncle helped me clean the shell. Now it has the same color as the back of my eyelids when I look at the sun with my eyes closed. I somehow managed to smuggle the shell safely through Bosnia, Croatia, Slovenia, and Austria back to Germany without the authorities finding it and taking it away from me.